For my children, Giselle and Brayden,
for being the light that guides me. —N. B.

To my parents, Florence and Guy.

To my brother, Louis, and my nephews and nieces who will enjoy
reading this book as much as I enjoyed drawing it.

And to my love, Noé, for always supporting me and my art. —J. O.

Designed by Winnie Ho

Published by Disney Press, an imprint of Buena Vista Books, Inc. No part of this book may be reproduced or transmitted in any
form or by any means, electronic or mechanical, including photocopying, recording, or by any information storage and retrieval
system, without written permission from the publisher. For information address Disney Press, 1200 Grand Central Avenue,
Glendale, California 91201.

Printed in the United States of America
First Hardcover Edition, October 2021
10 9 8 7 6 5 4 3 2 1
FAC-034274-21239
ISBN 978-1-368-07118-5
Library of Congress Control Number: 2021932127
For more Disney Press fun, visit www.disneybooks.com

Inspired by

Disney

ENCANTO

Antonio's Amazing Gift

Written by Naibe Reynoso   Illustrated by Juliette Oberndorfer

Disney PRESS

Los Angeles • New York

Antonio Madrigal lived in a magical house called **Casita**.

It was a big day at Casita. It was **Antonio's fifth birthday!** It was also his Gift Day.

The Madrigals each had a **special gift** and a **magical bedroom** to match.

His cousin *Luisa* had **super strength.**

His big sister, Dolores, could **hear** a pin drop from a mile away.

And his oldest cousin, Isabela, grew flowers with every step.

Antonio's family gathered around his **new bedroom door** and waited to see what his gift would be.

As Antonio touched the doorknob, a friendly-looking **toucan** appeared on his arm.

Squawk! Squawk!

"Yes, I **understand you.** Of course they can come," said Antonio.

It was his gift! He was able to **talk** with **animals.**

Abuela Alma hugged Antonio tight.
"I knew you could do it."

His new room was an **endless rain forest**. There was so much to see! The animals took turns showing him around.

First he watched as the **coatis** went **running** and **swinging** through the trees.

Then the **macaws** joined him high in the air for a bird's-eye view of his room below.

He even joined the
chigüiros for a snack.

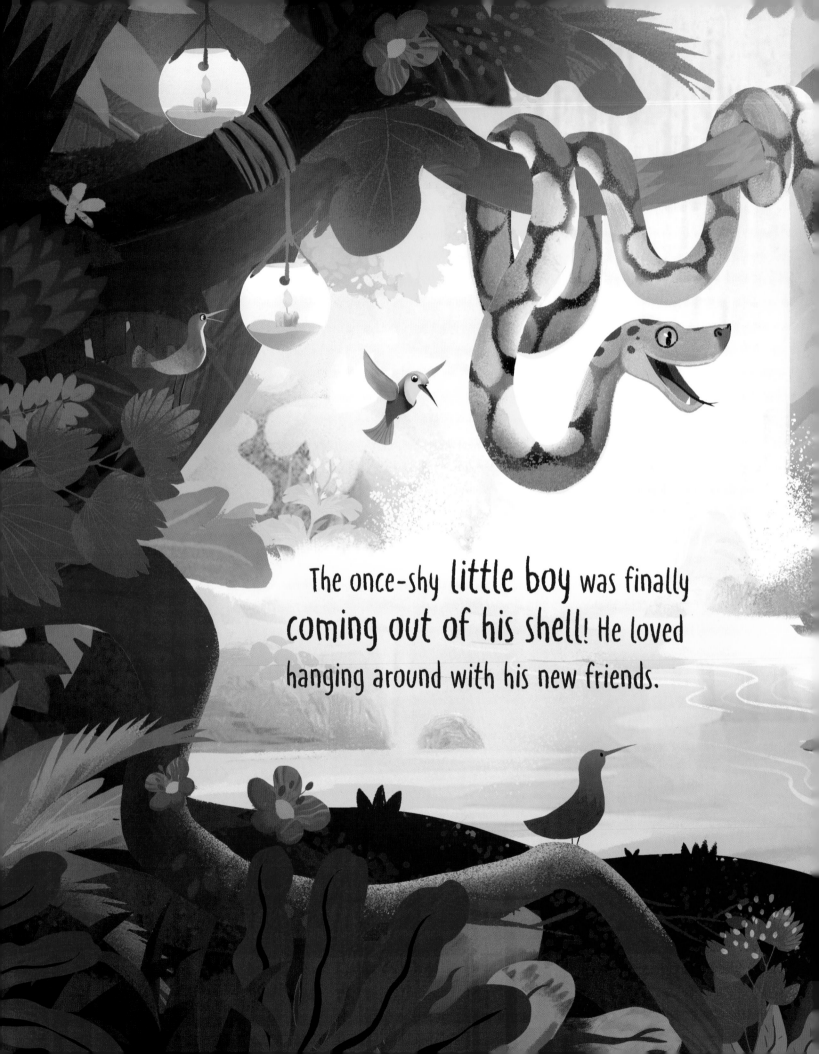

The once-shy **little boy** was finally **coming out of his shell!** He loved hanging around with his new friends.

And his new friends loved hanging around with Antonio. It was the best birthday ever!

Soon Antonio's family brought the rest of the birthday celebration to his room. The Madrigals looked around with their eyes wide in wonder. It was a room like no other in Casita!

Luisa brought the biggest plate of cocadas
Antonio had ever seen.
"We can help you with that!" he said.

His aunt, Julieta, had cooked arepas. The macaws helped themselves.

The entire family **danced** and **celebrated** Antonio's gift.

With all the fun he was having,
Antonio had lost track of time.
"It's almost **bedtime**," said
Antonio's mom.

Antonio let out a big yawn.
Soon all the animals were yawning, too.

"Good night!
¡Buenas noches!" said
Antonio, falling asleep in
his new room, surrounded
by new friends.